MW00885718

The Tale of Noodle the Uncurly Poodle

Katherine Lerner
Illustrated by Brelyn Giffin

Noodle was an adorable little Poodle, but he didn't think so……

…because Noodle looked different than the other Poodles who had curly, fluffy coats.

One day, Noodle was out walking with his human, Adella, when they came upon a Poodle Beauty Shop.

"Look at them Adella," exclaimed Noodle. "They're all so beautiful and happy. And there's Maxine, Billy's Poodle. The one in the back with the pink bow." Noodle thought she was very pretty.

"Adella," asked Noodle, "I'm a real Poodle, aren't I?"

"Yes Noodle," said Adella, "Of course you are a real Poodle."

"Then why don't I look like they do?" asked Noodle.

"Because," said Adella, "you were made differently, Noodle. You have a beautiful, smooth and shiny coat, and you are precious and lovable as you are."

Noodle suddenly became very upset.

"No! No Adella," he exclaimed. "I don't have curly fur like they do! If I had a curly coat I'd be beautiful, and then I'd be happy just like they are."

"Adella, please help me," begged Noodle. "I want to go to Sam the Sorcerer. He's a magician, and I know he can help me get a curly coat."

So off they went to Sam the Sorcerer.

"Ok Noodle," said Sam. "If you want a curly coat, you must drink this potion. It won't taste good, but if you drink it tonight, I promise you will have your curly coat in the morning."

So that night, Adella gave Noodle the magic drink.
Although it tasted terrible, Noodle quickly lapped it up.

Noodle wished Adella a good night and quickly curled
up in his bed, excited for the morning when he was
sure he would have his curly coat and be as happy as
the other Poodles.

The next morning Noodle awoke early and anxiously ran to the mirror to see his new curly coat. He was immediately horrified.

"YIKES! My hair is all SPIKES!!! ADELLA COME QUICK!" screamed Noodle. "I look like a porcupine! What am I going to do??"

"Oh my, Noodle!" said Adella as she saw Noodle, and matched his surprised look.

"Well," she said, trying to be calm, "we will just go back to Sam and have him fix this."

So Adella and Noodle returned to Sam the Sorcerer. Noodle felt sad as Sam looked at him and pondered what could have gone wrong.

"Hmmm," said Sam. "Well, even magicians make mistakes. I think I used too much Deer's Tongue and not enough Dragon's Blood."

Sam handed a small bottle to Adella.

"Just have him drink this tonight, and the prickly fur will be gone," said Sam. "Ok Noodle, now you will have that curly coat you want so badly."

That evening, Adella poured the potion into Noodle's bowl, and Noodle drank it in one gulp.

Noodle felt very anxious that night. He hoped that tomorrow would be the day he finally got his curly coat.

The next morning, he again woke early and ran to the mirror.

"Oh my gosh!" he shrieked. "Adella come quick! I look freaky. Worse than before! Now I'm a striped porcupine!"

Noodle felt very discouraged and sobbed. Adella tried so hard to comfort him.

"Don't worry Noodle," said Adella. "We will solve this somehow. Let me think a moment."

"Adella," said Noodle sadly, "I want so much to be the dog I used to be. I don't care about a curly coat anymore."

Adella ran to the other room and returned with
a newspaper.

"Look Noodle," said Adella. "I saw this ad in the
Collieville Gazette for Wes the Wizard. Maybe he can
help us."

"Oh I don't know Adella," said Noodle. "I'm just not
sure these magic people know what they're doing."

"Noodle," said Adella, "we have to trust that Wes can
help us."

Trying hard to be hopeful, Noodle and Adella went to the studio of Wes the Wizard.

"Hello there, Noodle," said Wes. "You don't like the way you look. Is that the problem?"

"Yes," said Noodle. "I was born to be a Poodle with a smooth coat, but I wanted a curly coat. And NOW look at me."

"Well, do you know that you can be different and still be perfect?" asked Wes. "But don't you worry any longer Noodle. Let's get you back to being that perfect puppy you were meant to be."

"When I put this magic cloth over your head," said Wes, "say three times, 'I love my smooth and shiny coat, I love my smooth and shiny coat, I love my smooth and shiny coat.'"

Noodle felt scared and worried what he would do if Wes's magic didn't work.

He promised himself that if he could return to being the dog he was meant to be, he would never again wish to change himself.

Noodle followed Wes's instructions and repeated three times, "I love my smooth and shiny coat, I love my smooth and shiny coat, I love my smooth and shiny coat."

Wes waved his magic wand over Noodle and quickly
pulled off the magic blanket.

Noodle looked in the mirror. "Look Adella! It's me again," exclaimed Noodle happily.

"Yes, you're back, Noodle, and you are as beautiful as you always were," said Adella.

"Oh thank you Wes, thank you!" cried Noodle.

As Adella and Noodle happily toddled out of Wes's studio, Noodle saw Billy and his Poodle, Maxine, walking in. The last time he had seen Maxine, she was in the beauty shop with all the other curly haired Poodles.

"Hi Noodle," said Maxine happily.

"Maxine," asked Noodle curiously, "what are you doing here?"

"I'm here to have Wes get rid of this awful curly coat. I hate this thick curly fur. Can't even get a comb through it," said Maxine. "I want a smooth and shiny coat like yours."

After recovering from his surprise at hearing Maxine's plan, Noodle felt sad as he thought about the agony and disappointment that might lie ahead for Maxine. He looked up at Adella and said, "Oh Adella, I so wish we could all be happy with just what we have and who we were meant to be."

The End

Made in the USA
Middletown, DE
02 June 2021